Pippin's Big Jump

By Hilary Robinson
Illustrated by Sarah Warburton

Special thanks to our advisers for their expertise:

Adria F. Klein, Ph.D.
Professor Emeritus, California State University
San Bernardino, California

Susan Kesselring, M.A.
Literacy Educator
Rosemount-Apple Valley-Eagan (Minnesota) School District

PICTURE WINDOW BOOKS
Minneapolis, Minnesota

Levels for *Read-it!* Readers

- Familiar topics
- Frequently used words
- Repeating patterns

- New ideas
- Larger vocabulary
- Variety of language structures

- Challenges in ideas
- Expanded vocabulary
- Wide variety of sentences

- More complex ideas
- Extended vocabulary range
- Expanded language structures

A Note to Parents and Caregivers:

Read-it! Readers are for children who are just starting on the amazing road to reading. These beautiful books support both the acquisition of reading skills and the love of books.

The RED LEVEL presents familiar topics using common words and repeating sentence patterns.

The BLUE LEVEL presents new ideas using a larger vocabulary and varied sentence structure.

The YELLOW LEVEL presents more challenging ideas, a broad vocabulary, and wide variety in sentence structure.

The GREEN LEVEL presents more complex ideas, an extended vocabulary range, and expanded language structures.

When sharing a book with your child, read in short stretches, pausing often to talk about the pictures. Have your child turn the pages and point to the pictures and familiar words. And be sure to reread favorite stories or parts of stories.

There is no right or wrong way to share books with children. Find time to read with your child, and pass on the legacy of literacy.

Adria F. Klein, Ph.D.
Professor Emeritus
California State University
San Bernardino, California

First American edition published in 2005 by
Picture Window Books
5115 Excelsior Boulevard
Suite 232
Minneapolis, MN 55416
877-845-8392
www.picturewindowbooks.com

First published in Great Britain by Franklin Watts, 96 Leonard Street,
London, EC2A 4XD

Printed in the United States of America.

Library of Congress Cataloging-in-Publication Data
Robinson, Hilary, 1962-
Pippin's big jump / by Hilary Robinson ; illustrated by Sarah Warburton.
p. cm. — (Read-it! readers)
Summary: Pippin the penguin is afraid of jumping into the sea, but his mother helps him
find some courage.
ISBN 1-4048-0555-9 (hardcover)
[1. Courage—Fiction. 2. Penguins—Fiction. 3. Mother and child—Fiction.]
I. Warburton, Sarah, ill. II. Title. III. Series.
PZ7.R566175Pi 2004
[E]—dc22
2004007329

Some penguins are
afraid of the dark.

Some penguins are afraid
of creaking icebergs.

But this penguin, Pippin, was afraid of jumping into the sea!

"Come on, Pippin," said Mother Penguin gently. "Watch the other penguins."

Pippin watched nervously as they
jumped off the iceberg and played
in the cool blue sea.

"Why don't you try, Pippin?"
Mother suggested. Pippin stood
quietly, shaking with fear.

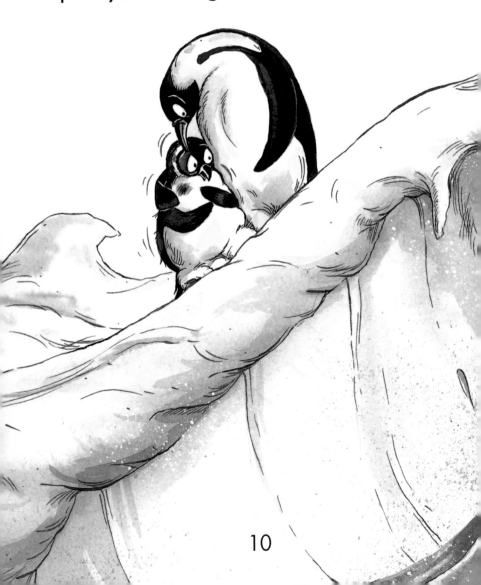

"Just try," said Mother. "I'll get into the water, and you can jump to me."

So Pippin said he would try.

He closed
his eyes.

He held his
breath.

He teetered
at the edge.

12

"After three, Pippin," called Mother.

"One, two, three, JUMP!"

"I can't. I'm too scared!"

Pippin sat down and cried.

"I'll never be a real penguin!"

"You are already," said Mother.

14

"No, I'm not!" cried Pippin.
"Real penguins swim and catch
fish. How can I catch fish if I'm too
scared to jump in the water?"

"It just takes courage," said Mother.

"What's courage?" asked Pippin.

"Can you hear a voice inside you

saying 'You can do it!' and another

voice saying 'No, you can't!'?
Courage is when you make the
'can do it' voice louder than the
'can't do it' voice," Mother explained.

"But it isn't easy, is it?" said Pippin.

"Well, I've got an idea!" Mother said.

"Sometimes courage is easier to find when we help each other. So why don't we all jump in together?"

Pippin liked that idea very much.

So Mother called the other young

penguins to the edge of the iceberg.

They all lined up, side by side.

"After three," called Mother.

"One, two, three, JUMP!"

In they jumped! Pippin dipped and dived and splashed and swam.

"Good job!" cheered Mother.

"You've done it, Pippin!"

Pippin was so happy. He loved playing in the water.

24

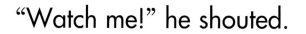

"Watch me!" he shouted.

"See how deep I can dive!"

25

And all the penguins
watched as Pippin
disappeared below
the waves. Then
they waited for
him to come
back up.

27

Mother was starting to worry. Then,

suddenly, up popped Pippin!

He scrambled on to the iceberg.

"What happened?" asked Mother.

"A fish," coughed Pippin.
"You caught your first fish on
your first swim? Good job!"
said Mother proudly.

"No!" said Pippin. "The fish tried to catch me!"

31

Levels for *Read-it!* Readers

**Read-it! Readers help children practice early reading
skills with brightly illustrated stories.**

Red Level: Familiar topics with frequently used words and
repeating patterns.

I Am in Charge of Me by Dana Meachen Rau
Let's Share by Dana Meachen Rau

Blue Level: New ideas with a larger vocabulary and a variety
of language structures.

At the Beach by Patricia M. Stockland
The Playground Snake by Brian Moses

Yellow Level: Challenging ideas with an expanded vocabulary
and a wide variety of sentences.

Flynn Flies High by Hilary Robinson
Marvin, the Blue Pig by Karen Wallace
Moo! by Penny Dolan
Pippin's Big Jump by Hilary Robinson
The Queen's Dragon by Anne Cassidy
Sounds Like Fun by Dana Meachen Rau
Tired of Waiting by Dana Meachen Rau
Whose Birthday Is It? by Sherryl Clark

Green Level: More complex ideas with an extended vocabulary
range and expanded language structures.

Clever Cat by Karen Wallace
Flora McQuack by Penny Dolan
Izzie's Idea by Jillian Powell
Naughty Nancy by Anne Cassidy
The Princess and the Frog by Margaret Nash
The Roly-Poly Rice Ball by Penny Dolan
Run! by Sue Ferraby
Sausages! by Anne Adeney
Stickers, Shells, and Snow Globes by Dana Meachen Rau
The Truth About Hansel and Gretel by Karina Law
Willie the Whale by Joy Oades

**A complete list of *Read-it!* Readers is available on our Web site:
www.picturewindowbooks.com**